10575761

THIS IS A BORZOI BOOK PUBLISHED BY ALFRED A. KNOPF, INC.

Copyright © 1989 by Anthony Browne. All rights reserved under International and Pan-American Copyright Conventions. Published in the United States by Alfred A. Knopf, Inc., New York. Distributed by Random House, Inc., New York. Originally published in Great Britain by Julia MacRae Books, a division of Walker Books Ltd., London. First American Edition.

Library of Congress Cataloging-in-Publication Data: Browne, Anthony. The tunnel/Anthony Browne.   p.   cm.   Summary: Scornful of his younger sister's fears, a young boy decides to explore a tunnel, forcing her to go after him when he doesn't return.   ISBN 0-394-84582-X   ISBN 0-394-94582-4 (lib. bdg.)   [1. Brothers and sisters—Fiction.   2. Fear—Fiction]   I. Title.   PZ7.B81984Tu   1989   [E]—dc19   88-31923   Manufactured in Italy   10 9 8 7 6 5 4 3 2 1

THE TUNNEL

ANTHONY BROWNE

ALFRED A. KNOPF · NEW YORK

Once upon a time there lived a sister and brother who were not at all alike. In every way they were different.

The sister stayed inside on her own, reading and dreaming. The brother played outside with his friends, laughing and shouting, throwing and kicking, roughing and tumbling.

At night he slept soundly in his room. But she would lie awake, listening to the noises of the night. Sometimes he crept into her room to frighten her, for he knew that she was afraid of the dark.

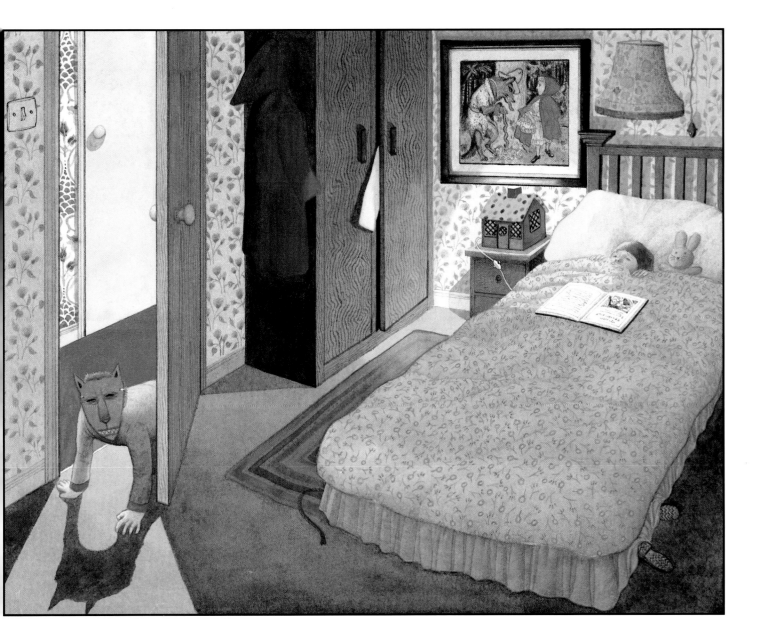

Whenever they were together they fought and argued noisily.
All the time.

One morning their mother grew impatient with them. "Out you go together," she said, "and try to be nice to each other just for once. And be back in time for lunch." But the boy didn't want his little sister with him.

They went to an empty lot.

"Why did you have to come?" he moaned.

"It's not my fault," she said. "I didn't want to come to this awful place. It scares me."

"Oh, you baby," said her brother. "You're frightened of everything."

He went off to explore.

"Hey! Come here!" he yelled a little while later. She walked over to him.

"Look!" he said. "A tunnel! Come on, let's see what's at the other end."

"N-no, you mustn't," she said. "There might be witches…or goblins…or *anything* down there."

"Don't be such a wimp," said her brother. "That's kid stuff."

"We have to be back by lunchtime…" she said.

His sister was frightened of the tunnel and so she waited for him to come out again. She waited and waited, but he did not come. She was close to tears. What could she do? She *had* to follow him into the tunnel.

The tunnel was dark,

and damp, and slimy, and scary.

At the other end she found herself in a quiet wood. There was no sign of her brother. But the wood soon turned into a dark forest. She thought about wolves and giants and witches, and wanted to turn back, but she could not — for what would become of her brother if she did? But now she was very frightened and she began to run, faster and faster…

Just when she knew she could run no farther,
she came to a clearing.
There was a figure, still as stone.
It was her brother.
"Oh no!" she sobbed. "I'm too late."

She threw her arms around the cold hard form, and wept. Very slowly, the figure began to change color, becoming softer and warmer.

Then, little by little, it began to move. Her brother was there.
"Rose! I knew you'd come," he said. They ran back, through
the forest, through the wood, into the tunnel, and out again.
Together.

When they reached home, their mother was setting the table.
"Hello," she said, "you two seem very quiet.
Is everything all right?"
Rose smiled at her brother.
And Jack smiled back.